Just Like MOMMY

Grosset & Dunlap

For *my* mommy, with love — M.E.B.

I love you Hannah Banana!
Much love & many thanks, Nee Nee & Papa — S.P.

Text copyright © 2003 by Megan E. Bryant. Illustrations copyright © 2003 by Stacy Peterson.
All rights reserved. Published by Grosset & Dunlap, a division of Penguin Putnam Books for
Young Readers, 345 Hudson Street, New York, NY, 10014. GROSSET & DUNLAP is a trademark
of Penguin Putnam Inc. Published simultaneously in Canada. Manufactured in China.

Library of Congress Cataloging-in-Publication Data is available.

ISBN 0-448-43107-6   A B C D E F G H I J

Just Like MOMMY

By Megan E. Bryant

Illustrated by Stacy Peterson

Grosset & Dunlap • New York

When Mommy was a little girl,
she was just like you—
she went to school, played games,
and had a mommy, too.

Though Mommy's all grown up now,
and you're the little kid,
it's fun to see the things you do
that once your mommy did!

You like to roller skate . . .

just like Mommy.

From: Megan
To: Mary Lou
Subject: Hi

How's scho

You write letters to your friends . . .

just like Mommy.

You love to chat on the phone . . .

just like Mommy.

just like Mommy.

You go to parties . . .

just like Mommy.

just like Mommy.

You get fancy haircuts . . .

just like Mommy.

You like eating in restaurants . . .

just like Mommy.

SALE!

BACK to School

You love buying new clothes . . .

just like Mommy.

Back to School

You love to read books . . .

just like Mommy.

You like frozen dinners . . .

just like Mommy.

You love amusement parks . . . .

just like Mommy.

You like to get dressed up . . .

just like Mommy.

Someday you'll be a grown-up,
just like Mommy is today.
And chances are that as you grow,
you'll change along the way.
But one thing always stays the same,
even as you grow—
Mommy will love you forever,
more than you'll ever know.